For more information, please contact:
Mascot Books
560 Herndon Parkway #120
Herndon, VA 20170
info@mascotbooks.com

All University of Georgia indicia are protected trademarks or registered trademarks of University of Georgia and are used under license.

CPSIA Code: PRT1112D
ISBN: 1932888462
ISBN-13: 9781932888461

Printed in the United States

How 'Bout Them Dawgs!

Vince Dooley

Illustrated by Miguel De Angel

MASCOT BOOKS

It was football season again at the
University of Georgia. Hairy Dawg
was on his way to Sanford Stadium.

He ran into some Bulldog fans
at the Arches. The fans cheered,
"How 'bout them Dawgs!"

Hairy Dawg visited alumni and fans
at Georgia parties all around town.

Hairy Dawg met a family of Bulldogs
outside their camper. They cheered,
"How 'bout them Dawgs!"

Hairy Dawg headed to the bookstore
to find some Georgia souvenirs.

The bookstore worker cheered,
"How 'bout them Dawgs!"

Hairy Dawg joined the football players
for the DawgWalk through campus.

As the players passed by,
they cheered,
"How 'bout them Dawgs!"

Hairy Dawg joined the team in the locker room before the big game.

The coach gave the team final
instructions and cheered,
"How 'bout them Dawgs!"

The players touched the
Uga statue as they ran
"Between the Hedges."

The team cheered,
"How 'bout them Dawgs!"

The Georgia Bulldogs scored
four touchdowns in the first half.

The referee thought,
How 'bout them Dawgs!

At halftime, the Redcoat Band took
the field and marched into formation.

After a great performance,
the band members cheered,
"How 'bout them Dawgs!"

It was now time for a cheer. One side of the stadium cheered, "GEORGIA!" then the other side cheered, "BULLDOGS!"

Hairy Dawg went into the stands to greet some of his friends. His friends said, "How 'bout them Dawgs!"

Georgia won the football game!
The players dumped water on the
coach to celebrate the victory.

The team threw Hairy Dawg
high into the air and cheered,
"How 'bout them Dawgs!"

After the game, Hairy Dawg joined
many Georgia fans at the Chapel for
the traditional ringing of the victory bell.

As fans and Coach Dooley
rang the bell, they cheered,
"How 'bout them Dawgs!"

For Georgia Fans, young and old, especially my grandchildren: Patrick, Catherine, Michael, Christopher, Ty, Matthew, Joe, John Taylor, Cal, Peyton, and Julianna ~ Vince Dooley

For Sue, Ana Milagros, and Angel Miguel ~ Miguel De Angel

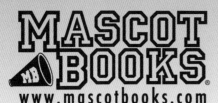

SCHOOL PROGRAM

Promote reading. Build spirit. Raise money.™

Mascot Books® is creating customized children's books for public and private elementary schools all across America. Containing school-specific story lines and illustrations, our books are beloved by principals, librarians, teachers, parents, and of course, by young readers.

Our books feature your mascot taking a tour of your school, while highlighting all the things and events that make your school community such a special place.

The Mascot Books Elementary School Program is an innovative way to promote reading and build spirit, while offering a fresh, new marketing or fundraising opportunity.

Starting Is As Easy As 1-2-3!

1 You tell us all about your school community. What makes your school unique? What are your well-known traditions? Why do parents and students love your school?

2 With the information you share with us, Mascot Books creates a one-of-a-kind hardcover children's book featuring your school and your mascot.

3 Your book is delivered!

Great new fundraising idea for public schools!

Innovative way to market your private school to potential new students!